Thanks for joining us on this KridderKiddz™ learning adventure!

Each KridderKiddz storybook...

- 🐸 Begins with a short and simple story designed to make young children think about a life concept.

- 🐸 Creates a safe space for your child to share thoughts and feelings about the subject. No judgment. No shaming.

- 🐸 Is hand illustrated in a unique watercolor style that young children relate to.

- 🐸 Centers around a design of brightly colored, hand-poured acrylic paints that engages kids.

- 🐸 Is filled with love by Just2Grandmas™!

To share or not to share. That is the question...

In this simple story children learn that sharing is a personal choice. But it goes both ways! Your friends can also choose to share... or not.

Tabby's Trampoline

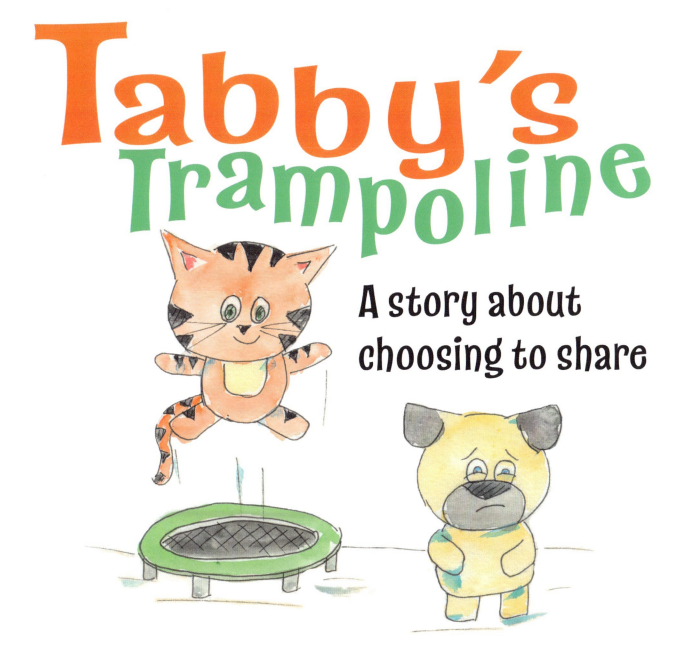

A story about choosing to share

Written and Illustrated by Just2Grandmas™

Daene Ruth, Author

Jane Marie, Illustrator

Copyright © 2022, Bright Child Learning, LLC.
All rights reserved.

You want to help your child learn and we want to provide tools that can help. If you purchased this book, you may reproduce individual pages or snippets of content (guilt free) to assist in your child's learning, as long as you do not attempt to profit from it or benefit commercially. If you share snippets or previews of it on social media or any other medium, including print, please include these credits: "© BrightChildLearning.com, Bright Child Learning, LLC."

Visit BrightChildLearning.com for more titles and learning ideas.

Written by Daene Ruth
Illustrated by Jane Marie

Dedicated to our beautiful grandchildren and to "kiddz" everywhere. Your innate desire to share is only surpassed by your enthusiasm for life that inspires us each and every day.

My name is Tabby.

I have a trampoline.

I like to jump on my trampoline.

I have a friend.

His name is Puggs.

I like my friend.

My friend Puggs
likes to jump
on my trampoline.

Sometimes...
I don't feel like sharing
my trampoline.

Sometimes...
when I don't share
my friend Puggs feels sad.

My friend Puggs has a skateboard.

He likes to ride his skateboard.

I like to ride his skateboard.

Sometimes...
my friend Puggs doesn't
feel like sharing.

Sometimes...
I feel angry
when he doesn't share.

But sometimes...
we share.

Remember...
You are in charge of you.

And you can choose
just what to do.

Parents and Teachers

If you wish to open a dialog about choosing to share, please continue.

This is the section
of thoughtful questions...

- Do you have a favorite toy?

- Do you sometimes choose to share your toy?

- Do you sometimes choose not to share your toy?

- How do you feel when you choose to share?

- How do you feel when you choose not to share?

- How do you feel when your friends choose to share?

- How do you feel when your friends choose not to share?

Jot a thoughtful note about what you learned together...

_____

_____

_____

_____

_____

_____

_____

_____

_____

_____

_____

Other KridderKiddz™ Learning Adventures...

- **My Best Friend is ME! -** A story about choosing to love and appreciate yourself

- **Zoey and the Green Chair -** A story about choosing how you feel about your world

- **The Grateful Book -** A story about choosing gratitude and feeling thankful for everyday things

- **Pepper Practices Kindness -** A story about choosing small acts of kindness every day

Visit **Just2Grandmas.com** for more titles!

If you enjoyed this book, would you be so kind as to leave us a review if asked by Amazon? We take your input seriously and appreciate it more than we can express.

Printed in Great Britain
by Amazon